The
Unexpected Day
and
The Trust

Stories by Ronald Tomanio
Illustrated by Anne Wemple Marks

SPECIAL 💡 IDEAS

The Unexpected Day
and
The Trust

By Ronald Tomanio
Illustrated by Anne Wemple Marks

Author's dedication:
Dr. Mary and Ritchard, together at peace.

Artist's dedication:
Virginia Waller Wemple
May 26, 1913 – April 23, 2002

Dear Reader, these are wonderful stories. We hope that the
spiritual insights they inspire will cause you to forgive any cultural,
historical or calligraphic errors they may contain. This is a work of
fiction. References to historic figures are not intended to be
historically accurate, but simply to inspire spiritual contemplation.
Drawings were inspired by Chinese cut-paper designs. Chinese
calligraphy is included as a symbolic design element, but is
not intended to be read as text.

Stories © 2002 Ronald Tomanio all rights reserved.
Book layout & cover design by Justice St Rain
Illustrations © 2002 Anne Wemple Marks.
ISBN# 1-888547-11-1
Published by Special Ideas
PO Box 9 Heltonville, IN 47436
http://www.special-ideas.com
1-800-326-1197

Printed in the USA
14 12 10 08 06 05 02 1 2 3 4

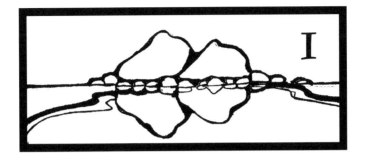

"YANTZ! WAKE UP NOW!" shouted Sien, Yantz's father. Finally, after vigorously shaking his head and showering his bed mat with beads of perspiration, Yantz woke up and slowly focused his eyes on his father's face.

"It was the same dream." Yantz whispered. "I dreamed that I saw my life's days unfold before my eyes. As a young man with my powers of body and mind at their highest, I began my journey well prepared for what I might find. I wore a warm coat to protect me from the winter winds. An animal skin bag of water hung from my shoulder and different small parcels of food were tied to my waist. As I aged, my back started to ache and my feet caused me great pain. I began to despair but I kept walking.

THE UNEXPECTED DAY

"One morning I woke up and the air was pleasantly warm. I stretched out my arms far into the future and my fingertips still felt only warmth. I took off my heavy coat and let it fall to the earth.

"The next morning I woke up with the sound of gently flowing water all around me. I climbed to the top of a large boulder and saw that the sparkling waters merged with the rays of the sun. I knew that I never need worry about thirst again. I took off from my shoulder my animal skin bag and let it drop to the earth. I walked all day along the banks of the stream stopping now and then to pick from the fruit trees that greeted me like old friends. I let my own parcels of food that had weighed me down fall to the earth. I continued to walk all day but I was very tired and my body was fading. I called out, 'How can I continue?'

"A voice answered, *'O my brother! Take thou the step of the Spirit.'* Then I awoke."

Father and son sat on pillows sipping hot tea until dawn. "Our family has always been chosen to dream the great dreams of our people. You must not break the golden thread to the other world. I think it is time for you to go out into the world and find the voice that calls to you. I sense that you will need great courage. It is a father's fear that compels me to suggest that you find a companion. How about your friend Wu? He is young and restless."

Sien got up slowly. "I am going back to bed. Adventures are for saplings, not for old trees like myself." Sien started to laugh. In fact, it was a rare moment when Yantz's father was not smiling or laughing.

After a restless night, Yantz had to restrain himself from calling too early at his friend's house. Wu's father, Chang, was an important and influential man. He was chief counselor to Nan-Su, the nephew of the emperor, who was the ruler of this province.

Yantz walked to the rear of the elaborate dwelling where he knew he would find Wu meditating in the courtyard. Without making a sound, Yantz sat down beside his friend and started to gaze at the arrangement of large rocks resting on a bed of tiny pebbles. It was all designed to be a peaceful window to one's inner world. Their long years of learning to quiet their minds allowed the melodies of the morning birds and the scent of jasmine to soothe their bodies while leaving their inner silence undisturbed. Wu was the first to stand up and speak.

"For many years I was listening to the silence. Now I silently listen."

"What do you hear, my brother?" asked Yantz.

"I hear an echo from the emptiness inside me. My life's book has been written for me. Not each word, thankfully, but certainly the plot. I have been trained in history, philosophy and medicine in order that I might heal the problems of the body, mind and spirit of the powerful. I will sit beside my father at Nan-Su's palace, and eventually take his place. Do you understand how my future scares me, Yantz?"

"There are many who would embrace your future, my friend, and the privileges and wealth that would accompany it, " Yantz replied. " I do, however, understand. I am expected to follow in my father's footsteps but they are still my shoes and I intend to make my own mark in this world. That is why I have come to you. My time as an oracle has arrived. I have received my first great dream. My father assures me that this is only the beginning. I ask you to join me on my quest." Yantz went on to relate his great dream to Wu and how the voice urged him to take the first step on the path of search. "I must be honest with you Wu. I can only promise you mystery, danger, and the unexpected."

"I will go with you. This is the answer to all my prayers. I will explain all this to my father and join you tomorrow morning," Wu decided with great conviction.

That night Wu and his father quarreled bitterly. "I am an old man. My time of service to the emperor's family is drawing to a close. You must take my place or you will forever disgrace our family!" The tall angular Chang was trembling with anger.

"I cannot do it! I cannot live your life all over again!" an equally angry Wu responded.

"What is wrong with my life and our place as counselors to the rulers? It is an honorable profession!" fired back Chang.

"Father, I know you to be a good and wise man, but just as the preparers of the dead clothe the privileged in the finest of silks and most aromatic of scents, you are forced to sheath the evil deeds of your masters in eloquent but hollow words." Wu knew the second he had said these harsh words that the heat of the moment had caused him to strike too deep, but his youthful pride would now allow him to back down.

Wu's father turned white as though mortally poisoned. "Go, then. I no longer have a son." Then Chang retired to his private quarter.

The next morning Wu and Yantz were ready to go. Taking only what they could comfortably carry, they planned to work for their food and lodging. Wu glanced back over his shoulder.

"I know he will not come to say good-bye, but I must look for him anyway."

Sien addressed his son, "When you were a boy I would put rocks in your pockets and I would say, 'This will keep your feet on the ground.' I am tired of searching the clouds for you. Now I say it is time to take the rocks away and let you soar!"

Sien embraced his son and gave him a sum of money for emergencies. Sien then embraced Wu. "I will speak to your father when he calms down. Do not loose heart." He then gave Wu a sum of money.

ONE YEAR LATER...

"I am hungry, Yantz. Is there a village nearby where we can barter for food?"

"You would think, my well-born friend, that the rich fare of your childhood would still suffice," countered Yantz with the slyest of smiles.

"My wise, all-seeing friend should know that memory makes a poor meal."

"Enough," laughed Yantz. "You can win the battle of wits but I would rather win the war of empty stomachs."

The two men, each in their early twenties, were a lot alike. Both had restless hearts that beat faster when they approached the top of the hill, excited about what new wonders they would see on the other side.

THE UNEXPECTED DAY

Yantz and Wu had been walking all day and were anxious about finding food and shelter as they reached the crest of a small hill. They saw a fisherman sitting on the banks of a stream in obvious distress. The closer they came to him, the louder his moans grew. The two friends could see a nearby village, but it was too far away for anyone to hear his cries for help. As they ran down the hill, they realized the fisherman was bleeding. While they approached, the injured man pleaded, "I have cut my leg very deeply with my cleaning knife and am bleeding badly. Please take me to my village." He tried to get to his feet but collapsed on the bank of the stream.

"Calm yourself friend. I am skilled in the ways of healing," said Wu as he applied pressure above a deep gash in the man's thigh. "Yantz, take my place. Hold your hands tight above the wound. It will decrease the loss of blood while I gather herbs and flowers."

"Please save me, and my life is yours!" cried the fisherman.

"I am trying!" assured Yantz. His knuckles were turning white from squeezing the man's leg so forcefully.

Wu, belying his frail academic appearance, moved nimbly about the area gathering healing plants and adding powdered herbs from his satchel. He quickly stanched the bleeding and bandaged the man's leg. "You can release your hands, Yantz. Well, my fisherman friend, I think you will survive. The wound was more bloody than dangerous."

Wu sat down on the stream bank and splashed his sweating face.

"Kind doctor, you are too modest. You have saved my worthless life! My name is Lan and my home lies in that nearby village," said the fisherman, pointing to the simple bamboo and grass structures. "Please, great healer Wu and his noble assistant Yantz, be the guests of my humble family."

Lan hopped on the strong back of Yantz while Wu gathered the fishing poles and fish. Wu began to laugh, "What a strange sight we must be. If my father could see me now he would disown me again."

"You have already been disowned once. I do not believe it is possible to be disowned twice," replied a huffing and puffing Yantz.

"I have discovered it's painful to laugh while carrying a wounded fisherman on my back!"

"How is it, Yantz, that we can be so happy even though we have thrown the world away for a dream?"

"Perhaps that is a suitable definition of happiness," a suddenly serious Yantz opined.

That night the whole village honored Wu and Yantz as heroes and celebrated by giving a feast for them. Everyone gathered around a bonfire in an open space reserved for such important meetings. Even the village elder, who rarely left his hut anymore, wanted to address the people. His two grandsons helped him to stand close enough to the fire to be warmed on this cool spring night.

"A long time ago," he said, "there was a mighty warrior who defeated an evil warlord in battle. The people hailed him and called him 'hero' but inside they were all afraid of this man because he had taken away life. The hero grew to know this fact and he left searching for his next battle and the brief moments of adulation that he hoped would follow. Now you young men have given life, not taken it away. Therefore there is

no fear in our hearts, only love, and it is my wish that the people of this village look upon Wu and Yantz with my very old eyes— eyes so cloudy with age that I am never quite sure who is a member of my family and who is not." The elder paused and held out his arms as if trying to embrace them all. "Therefore I am compelled to love everyone." The elder walked back to his lodging leaning on his grandson while the people nodded and looked warmly at Wu and Yantz. As the evening wore down, Lan invited his two saviors back to his dwelling.

"My family is your family. My wife, Ling, is your sister. Our daughters, Ji and Jen, are your nieces and I am your brother. This will always be true no matter how far you travel."

"Thank you, Lan, we are honored," offered Wu. "If I ever resume my career as a counselor, I will remember the wisdom of the people of this village."

After their hosts left, Yantz, who had been strangely quiet all night, looked around the simple dwelling for the best place to unfurl his bedroll. Wu, however, was too exhilarated by the day's events to want to go to sleep just yet. "I want to thank you for this day, Yantz."

THE UNEXPECTED DAY

After some moments of silence Yantz answered, "There is no need. You saved the life of the fisherman. I was only your humble assistant."

Wu struggled to lift his thoughts over a wall of emotion. "I find it so difficult to explain what I am feeling. This past year has been filled with days that I did not know existed. One after another they have been unexpected days taking me by complete surprise. I do not know if I can go back to my old predictable life. I know I sound like a fool, but while we have these adventures, I keep thinking that if I were home my day would have all been planned out for me!" Wu bowed his head. "My future confuses me and I am in need of your counsel."

"Do not take offense at what I am about to tell you," Yantz responded, "but I take solace in your upheaval. It makes me feel less alone in my own swirling soul. Sometimes when we walk through the countryside everything changes. I find myself standing in a vast desert, all alone. Nothing moving, not one spec of sand...and on the horizon...a solitary tree with shimmering leaves urging me on. We are brothers in confusion," laughed Yantz. "You have not been following a wise guide but one whose longings have brought him to the edge of madness.

"I do have some advice, however. My father told me before I left not to let go of the golden thread to the other world. If you do this also, your life will be an unfoldment of wonder no matter where you live or what you must do outwardly. Now I am surrounded by sleep and I must surrender."

"I will think deeply about what you have told me. I feel like taking a walk around the village before retiring. Goodnight, Yantz," but Yantz did not answer because he was already asleep. While walking, Wu thought about the life he had left behind and his father. The warmth of the remains of the bonfire attracted him and he sat down on a nearby log. He whispered in the direction of what he thought was home, "Does your heart still smolder like the embers of this fire, my father? Will I ever see you again and will you ever call me 'Son' again?"

Wu heard no answers to his questions, only the faint sound of a rushing stream off in the distance and the nearby cry of a baby hungry for its mother.

Finally, exhaustion overcame excitement and Wu felt a strong need to sleep. He entered the hut as quietly as he could so he would not disturb Yantz but, to his amazement, he found

Yantz standing perfectly still with his hands covering his face.

Wu had seen his friend like this before and he knew what to do. He stood silently next to Yantz, ready in case he lost his balance.

Yantz's hands fell to his side. "People, what is wrong with you? Would you take the blue from the sky or the song from the nightingale's throat?" Yantz fell to his knees. "I don't want to see this anymore. The pain is more than I can bear."

Wu became frightened. Whatever his friend was going through was tearing him apart. Wu started shaking Yantz's shoulders very hard.

"Yantz! Wake up now!" he shouted over and over again. At last Wu could tell by the look in his friend's eyes that he was free of the vision. Wu helped Yantz to a chair and waited for him to speak.

"He was being led through the streets in chains. His long black hair was tinged with blood. The crowd was throwing stones and screaming curses. I couldn't stand to look and was about to turn away when suddenly he stopped and raised his arm. It was a gesture of an all-powerful King. The mob parted as if they were now under his control. An old woman who had not been able to get close enough to throw her stone now had a clear view of the prisoner. He spoke a few words to her in a gentle manner and she responded with all the fury her frail form could muster. She hurled her rock and he made no attempt to avoid it. The sound when it hit him...I, I couldn't stand to watch anymore. I started screaming, 'Show me the way to your side and I will free you or die trying!'"

"Did he answer you?" asked Wu.

"I believe he did. The vision started to fade as these words filled my mind:

'O Son of Justice!
Whither can a lover go but to the land of his beloved? and what seeker findeth rest away from his heart's desire? To the true lover re-union is life, and separation is death. His breast is void of patience and his heart hath no peace. A myriad lives he would forsake to has-ten to the abode of his beloved.'*"

"What manner of man is this?" asked Wu.

---

*Bahá'u'lláh: Persian Hidden Words #4

"Not like us at all. He has the power of the sun but he veils it. All I wanted to do was bow down, but I knew he wanted me to watch and to remember."

Wu paced back and forth. "Yantz! We must find him and try to rescue him!"

"We must wait for inspiration," Yantz cautioned. "Our puny minds will not show us the way. He must reach out for us. Let us get some rest and talk in the morning. I have a strong feeling that we will need all our strength in the coming days."

Wu awoke with great eagerness to continue their quest, but Yantz was gone and only a note remained.

"The path has taken a dangerous turn," it said. "I do not have the right to risk your life, only my own. Please do not follow me. Return to your father."

Wu crumpled up the note and threw it to the ground. "Maybe when we began our journey a year ago, I was more interested in leaving home and having an adventure, but the fire of search burns bright in my own heart now, and nothing can stop me from following you." Wu realized that Lan and Ling were staring at him wondering whom he was talking to. Wu told them about Yantz's note, and tried to explain to his friends why he had to follow Yantz.

Lan and Ling begged him not to go but finally realized it was useless to try to stop him.

"I will stay one more day to make sure your leg is healing properly," Wu reassured them. "Don't worry, I will show Ling how to change your bandage."

The next morning the whole village turned out to wish him a safe journey. Wu could hardly walk with all the food he was given. For the first time since he left home a year ago, Wu felt a terrible fear. He knew from experience that if Yantz sensed danger, it would surely come to pass.

MEANWHILE, as Wu was about to leave the small village, Yantz was entering a fairly large city on the Silk Road, an ancient trade route.

Yantz entered a market place active with exotic aromas and colors. Normally, he would have been curious about each stall, but he hadn't felt normal since his dream-vision two nights ago. The feeling of great danger was back, but instead of being repelled, he was strangely drawn deeper into the swirling crowd of buyers and sellers.

Suddenly the mass of people parted and bowed. A procession of soldiers bracketed a dark-haired figure who had gotten out of her carriage to walk alongside it. She was waving to the crowd who had never seen a royal princess look or act like this.

Two merchants whispered, "The emperor must wonder if he has a princess or a prince."

"That is the emperor's problem. It does not matter to me who I grovel before, I still must bow just as low," the other merchant responded.

Yantz rushed the line of soldiers, so surprising them that he broke their ranks. He flung himself at the dark-haired figure shouting, "People of ignorance! Do not harm this person anymore! He has suffered enough! Throw no more stones!"

The furious guards recovered quickly and started beating and kicking Yantz, who rolled to the ground screaming in pain.

"Stop!" commanded the princess Ming Tsai. "If he dies, you guards will take his place. A dead man cannot answer my questions." The princess addressed the head of her private guard, a massive man who picked up Yantz as if he were a bag of feathers. "Find out where this man came from and if he has any accomplices."

Two days later Wu entered the same ancient city. Following Yantz had proven to be an easy task. Villagers had no trouble remembering the stranger who asked for food and drink.

"He had a look in his eyes that no one had ever seen before," remarked one peasant.

Wu found the city still in a state of great agitation. The people were shocked that anyone would actually attack the daughter of the emperor. She was well known to be his favorite child. The emperor overlooked her bold habits of walking amongst the people dressed more like a soldier than a princess, and her many other eccentricities. The question on everyone's lips was, "Is this the act of a crazed individual or was he the agent of a larger group of conspirators?"

Wu's stomach was a bottomless pit of fear. "I feel it in my bones that they are talking about Yantz but this gentle soul has never harmed anyone in his life," he thought to himself. After asking what the attacker looked like and what he was wearing, Wu knew his intuition was correct.

He did not know where to turn. The only person who had the slightest influence with the authorities was his father who had disowned him. Even if he were willing to help, he lived over two hundred miles to the east in the province where he served as counselor to the emperor's nephew, Nan-Su.

He began to panic but realized there was no hope at all if he could not think clearly. Wu sat on a stone bench next to a well and made himself eat and drink. His long years of training spent gaining control of his emotions was sorely tested, but he gradually felt an old familiar calmness return.

"Try to think," he said, tapping his forehead. "Yantz believes he is a part of some divine plan. If he is correct there must be a way out of this dark alley. Yes! There must be a path." He concluded his inner conversation and then noticed a small boy with a water bucket looking all around obviously trying to discover who he was talking to. Wu patted the boy's shoulder. "Let me help you draw some well water, my little friend."

They had to wait their turn behind a very imposing man in a military outfit. "Wait a minute, I know that uniform, only the personal guard of Nan-Su wear those colors. If Nan-Su is here, that means his chief counselor, Chang, my father, is here!"

Wu looked around the market square and noticed many soldiers wearing different uniforms.

"There must be a conference of provincial rulers taking place in this city." Wu remembered that when he was a teenager his father had gone away for a month to such a conference. He decided to risk everything and tell all to the large guard.

"Pardon me, sir, my name is Wu, son of Chang, chief counselor to Nan-Su. The man who is in prison for attacking the princess is my best friend and traveling companion. We were separated at the village of Lan-Chou three days journey from here. Would you kindly take me to my father? I'm sure he would reward you."

The guardsman stood thinking for a second and then said, "I would be glad to help you. Come with me."

THE GUARDSMAN LED WU through narrow winding streets until at last they came to a stone building.

"This is a very foreboding conference site," he remarked to the guardsman. The soldier was talking to another soldier who was guarding the entrance gate. They were speaking so low that Wu could not hear the words.

"Come my young friend, let us go to your father and I shall collect an even greater reward from the emperor himself," boasted the soldier.

Before Wu could collect his spinning thoughts, he found himself thrown into a very large, dark prison cell with only one other inhabitant. Wu had to wait patiently before his eyes adjusted to the subterranean dimness. He saw a curled up figure by the wall that he knew must be Yantz. He walked over, afraid to see what condition his friend was in.

Wu knelt down beside Yantz and examined him, "Can you hear me?"

Yantz replies in a faint voice, "Yes, but it is hard for me to talk."

"You have been beaten very badly, you have some broken ribs and your eyes are swollen shut."

"Wu, I'm not afraid, my spirit soars! Some power has parted countless veils and allowed me to see!" Yantz tried to raise his head but began to cough violently.

"Lie still, my brother, they have not taken away my medicine bag. I can give you something for the pain." Wu took off his jacket and covered his friend up. He tore his shirt sleeves into strips and soaked them in an herb and water mixture and began cleaning the blood from Yantz's face. At the same time he looked around, his eyes now adjusting to the darkness. The room was spacious and could easily hold a hundred prisoners.

"They must think us very dangerous to keep us so isolated," Wu thought to himself. The only light in the room came from two oil lamps recessed into the stone wall on either side of the door. Wu sat exhausted with his back to the cold, stone wall. He looked at Yantz and just knowing that his friend was finally able to sleep without pain had a relaxing effect on his mind. He whispered to Yantz, "I wish I could see what you see, maybe then I wouldn't be so afraid."

The creaking of their cell door awoke Wu from a deep sleep. The guard brought their food and water and took back yesterday's dirty bowls. Wu tried to engage the guard in conversation but it was useless. Several mornings later, their eyes met and the guard's eyes seemed to say, "It would be dangerous for me to talk to you."

A different guard brought their evening meal and his rough manner signaled that the sooner they were executed the happier he would be. Yantz slowly regained his strength. The swelling around his eyes subsided and after about a week all his cuts and bruises were almost healed.

Wu gradually began to notice how different his friend had become. The fact that he had been brutally beaten, thrown into a cold dark prison cell, and at any moment would be taken away and executed, did not seem to cause him the slightest worry. Just the opposite, he had never known Yantz to be so happy and filled with life.

The next morning the guard came in with one side of his face swollen, trying to stifle a moan, "My friend, what troubles you? I am a trained healer and I have my medicine pouch."

"Speak softly, it is against the rules to talk to you, but I will surely lose my mind because of this pain," groaned the guard. Wu made a poultice of pain-killing herbs and applied it to the troublesome tooth. The grimace on the guard's face gradually began to fade.

"You have saved me, prisoner Wu. There is little I can do to help one facing execution, but if there is something..."

"Take a message to my father," interrupted Wu, "his name is Chang and he is counselor to Nan-Su. It is our only chance. I pray that he is still in the city."

The guard confirmed that the conference of provincial rulers was still going on and promised to try to contact Wu's father.

Wu gave him some coins that he had saved for an emergency and also instructions on what to do about his infected tooth. He glanced over at his sleeping friend and said in a low voice, "We have hope."

After the guard left, Wu woke up Yantz and told him what had happened.

A short while later the cell door opened and another prisoner was brought in. There were extra guards and one man who had the look of an important official. All the others deferred to him. "You will be executed tomorrow at dawn," he announced, and then left abruptly with the guards.

Wu rushed to put his arms around Lan who looked like a ghost. "I did nothing, great healer Wu," the fisherman said, "nothing...nothing.... The soldiers came and asked questions about two strangers. I freely admitted knowing you both and letting you stay overnight in my dwelling. They burned my hut down with all my possessions." Wu helped Lan sit down before he fell down.

"Did they harm Ling and the girls?" asked Wu.

"No, they are fine, they are with my parents."

"Wu...., " Lan's face reflected a frightened realization, that he may never see them again.

"Do not give up hope." Wu counseled, "I have managed to send word to my father and he is very influential." Wu spent the afternoon trying to convince Lan not to give up, that there were greater forces at work. They talked about Yantz's dream-visions and what they could mean. Finally Wu said, "I must confess that there is so much about this quest that remains a mystery to me, but I am convinced that there is a divine purpose behind everything that has happened." Suddenly Yantz, who had been sleeping most of the day, sat up and stared at the furthest and darkest corner of the cell. Wu, who had seen Yantz do this before, cautioned Lan to remain quiet and not talk to Yantz at all.

"But there is nothing..."

"There is Lan! We can't see...though we must be quiet." The faint light from the oil lamps caused the tears on Yantz's face to glisten.

Yantz's voice broke the long silence. "We must welcome our visitors."

Before Wu or Lan could say anything, they heard the lock mechanism on the door turn and standing in the doorway was their friendly morning guard and Wu's father, Chang.

Wu ran to embrace his father, saying, "Forgive me, Father."

"Only if you will forgive me, my son. It's hopeless you know, princess Ming Tsai is beyond my influence."

"It is not hopeless," said Yantz getting to his feet but holding his arms tightly around his broken ribs, "tell the princess to come tonight and I will prove to her that my story is true!"

"This is preposterous, Ming Tsai would never come to a prison cell. Are you mad, Yantz?"

Yantz replied to Chang calmly, "Tell her I know that the emperor is dying, and he has secretly named her as his successor."

"What?" bellowed Chang. "I have been at this conference for three weeks. Everyone says that the emperor's oldest son is going to succeed his father and besides, the emperor is only slightly ill."

"Listen to Yantz, Father," begged Wu. "Our lives depend upon it."

That night through the intercession of Nan-Su, the princess's first cousin, Chang gained an audience with her. He mused to himself, "How strange – that courage would pay me a visit this late in life. I only hope it stays the entire evening."

Chang was ushered into the presence of the princess. She was painting a portrait of the emperor. Her long, black luxurious hair fell to her waist. The contrast of pale skin framed by black hair was striking.

"Your Highness, I am grateful for the chance to speak for my son and his friends," a bowing Chang went on to tell her about their quest and of the dream-visions of Yantz that led Yantz to mistakenly think that her Highness was the figure in his dreams.

"So you see, in his mind, he was merely trying to protect you from a stoning by the crowd."

Ming Tsai put down her paintbrush. She admired her artistry for a moment before looking at Chang.

"My cousin has said you have served him faithfully for many years. Nan-Su has also told me that you have a clever and nimble mind. The compliment does not go far enough. You really expect me to believe this fantasy, Chang? I can understand a father's attempt to save the life of his son and I bear you no ill will, but please leave before you exhaust my benevolence." The princess calmly picked up her brush and dipped it into a small jar of paint. Her gaze shifted from Chang back to the painting as two burly guards approached Chang.

"If you will dismiss your guards, I will give you proof, I have a message from Yantz meant for only your ears."

Ming Tsai sat tapping the arm of her chair with her fingers. "Guards dismissed!" she ordered. "You have crossed over the edge, Chang. Fail to convince me and you will join your son!"

Chang paused and looked around to make sure they were alone. "Your father, the emperor, is dying and he has named you his successor. You will be the first woman to lead this great land."

Chang did not need a verbal reply to know his words were true. What little color she had in her face totally vanished. Her paintbrush fell to the floor splattering tiny droplets of brown paint on the hem of her white silk robe. She clutched the arms of her chair so hard that her arms turned bloodless. She pulled a cord hanging down from the ceiling without taking her eyes off Chang. A guard appeared.

"Bring my carriage around. We leave immediately for the prison!"

ALL WAS QUIET until they were alone in her carriage riding to the prison over narrow cobblestone streets.

"This oracle of yours has cheek. Luckily for him, I like cheek. I must warn you, however, that you will all die as planned at dawn if I am not utterly convinced."

Chang made no reply. It was up to Yantz now.

The sleepy guard at the prison gate had trouble believing his eyes. Princess Ming Tsai and her private guard were walking straight toward him. While ten steps away, she shouted, "Open!"

The guard hurriedly tried to unlock the front gate and bow at the same time.

"Summon the warden at once!" The guard ran off and in a minute returned with the warden who looked petrified.

THE UNEXPECTED DAY

The warden started babbling nonsensically about what an honor it was to have her in his prison. "Of course, I don't mean as a prisoner, your Highness, I didn't mean to imply...that is, we are honored..."

"Shut up, you fool, and take me to the cell of the three conspirators."

When they got to the cell door she commanded, "Only Chang and I will enter. If I shout for help, come immediately."

The warden tried to urge caution, "They are dangerous criminals, your Highness."

The princess ignored his warnings and went into the cell. Chang followed, his heart beating loudly in his thin chest.

She walked up to Yantz, who did not rise and bow like Wu and Lan. She said, "I am ready to be utterly convinced."

"You'll need to sit next to me and remain quiet," said Yantz serenely.

"Now, that is courage," thought Chang to himself.

A stillness fell upon the room. "This is outrageous," the princess started to say, but she was interrupted by the most beautiful chanting any human being had ever heard.

The princess sat down next to Yantz with her back against the wall, as did Wu, Chang and Lan. They sat, they listened, and they waited.

After a few moments, a pin dot of light appeared in the furthest section of the cell. It began to expand vertically and horizontally. As the light expanded, the chanting grew louder. The light hurt eyes that were unaccustomed to such brightness, but as their eyes adjusted they began to discern shapes. Eventually, they could see two rows of men, heavily chained, facing one another.

In amazement, Wu glanced back at Yantz. There were tears running down his cheeks. Wu realized that his friend had seen this before. His gaze returned to the rows of men enveloped by an incredible light that had the scent of roses. A guard appeared from the darkness behind one man and put his hand on his shoulder. He was released from his chains and literally danced with ecstasy over to a figure Who glowed so brightly it was difficult to look at Him for more than a moment. They embraced and the prisoner was led away into the darkness by the guard.

Nothing could have prepared them for what happened next. The glowing man in their vision then raised his right arm and beckoned Yantz to take the now vacant spot in the rows of prisoners. Slowly and painfully, still clutching his damaged ribs, Yantz got to his feet. The long year of searching was over. But when He tried to move forward, he collapsed in a heap. He trembled in anger at his broken body. "I am so close, so astonishingly near...but I have no more strength," he whispered.

Wu rushed to his side. "You are too weak! You will kill yourself, Yantz!" Wu's heart was broken by the sight of his best friend weeping on the prison floor.

Yantz turned his head to speak to Wu. "Help me to my feet. He hasn't brought me this far...there must be a way!" It took all of Wu's strength to keep Yantz from falling again. Yantz cried out, addressing the radiant figure, "I tried to save the Savior of the world! I sought to bring a ladle of water to the ocean. There was no need to cross deserts and live in caves. All I had to do was open my arms and receive a gift. I stand powerless before you."

A voice replied with words that Yantz had heard almost a year ago, but now they were healing words that changed his life forever. "O my brother, take thou the step of the Spirit..."[*]

The words had not finished echoing in the cell when Yantz stopped clutching his ribs and started walking to take his place amongst the rows of prisoners. He had come home.

Wu and Lan received their call together and eagerly took their places next to Yantz.

Only the princess remained. Once again the glowing figure swept His arm through the blackness like a fiery comet. All became silent. The only sound was the sobbing of the princess who was now standing with her hands covering her face. "I...I am not worthy to be with you in the same world and yet you call me to take a place by your side."

A pathway of light extended out to meet the princess. Her legs took a few shaky steps and suddenly she knew what it was like to be led away to one's execution. She opened her eyes and knew what it was like to have nowhere to turn. She turned her head to listen and heard only the struggle of a heartbeat to survive an-

[*] Bahá'u'lláh: Kitáb-i-Íqán, The Book of Certitude pg. 43

other day, and when she was one step away from Him, her mind felt not the sorrow of broken dreams but the numbing pain of all those countless souls that could not dream at all.

Ming Tsai then collapsed onto the floor beside the others.

The chanting began again, only louder this time. There were two rows of prisoners, delirious with happiness. One row would chant, "God is sufficient unto us," and the other would answer, "In Him let the trusting trust."

At dawn the perplexed warden and his guards entered cautiously and prepared to carry out the orders of execution. What they found were four men and one woman sitting with their arms around one another.

The warden and the guards were frozen in bewilderment, not knowing what to do.

The princess stood up and announced, "There will be no dying today. Those men are innocent. Bring my carriage. We are all going back to the palace."

"One last thing: seal up this room forever after we leave. It will house no more prisoners."

SO MING TSAI did become the first empress of her country. She became known for her cosmopolitan view of the world.

Lan went back to his village and his favorite fishing spot.

Wu became a respected counselor, like his father Chang, but in his own distinct way. Years later, Wu would tell his wife that each day when he rose to greet the morning light, he was engulfed in a sea of rose scent and was carried throughout his waking hours on waves of chanting voices.

Yantz roamed his great country continuing to dream the dreams of his people, returning every so often when he sensed his friend Wu was in need of another unexpected day.

They continued to hold that night in common and, whether sleeping in a palace or a thatched hut, they continued to listen to the melody of astonishment and look for the light with the scent of roses.

The prison door remains sealed to this day, these many years later. If you should ever visit this ancient city on the "Silk Road" and were to wipe the dust off that same sealed cell door, you would read this poem by Ming Tsai:

Joyous sounds, like flowers in spring,
    escape their earthen prison
The rest of rulers is disturbed by the
    ceaseless chants of the King of Kings
The peace of the world was born
    in a manger of chains,
    the lightness of his youthful heart
    illumines the darkest of paths
So sing your songs and tell your stories
    to a world wet with tears,
And if sleep eludes you one troubled night,
    listen and remember
    the Laughter of Angels.

THE END

45

The following story, *The Trust,* is also available as a play for student theatre groups. Contact the publisher for more information.

L<small>I</small> LIVED A WONDERFUL LIFE surrounded by the security of massive castle walls
and the beauty of formal gardens. Li was
shielded from the slightest discomfort by his
only two living relatives, his father, and his
great aunt.

Li's father was the powerful general Tso, Commander of Armies, and the ruler of a vast kingdom. Great Aunt Pei was his constant companion and teacher. It was the tradition of
these people that the old should teach the
young. The children received knowledge and
the old ones gained wisdom in exchange.

Great Aunt Pei used words sparingly. She
would say that there has to be a good reason to
disturb the beauty of silence. Indeed Great
Aunt Pei spent much time in silent contempla-

tion and even her movements were soundless. Li would watch from his bedroom as she took her twilight walk in the gardens. It was like a painting that came to life. They shared a common attribute, neither one was afraid of Li's father. Li had noticed that everyone else lived in fear of the all-powerful warlord.

Today was a lonely day. His father had been gone for months fighting a great battle, and tomorrow would be Li's seventh birthday. The General had never failed to be home on his son's birthday.

"Come boy, let us walk together in the gardens and I will tell you marvelous stories; perhaps I can make the sadness leave your eyes," said Great Aunt Pei.

"Only if you speak to me again of my Great Uncle Wu," Li answered.

As they walked past live peacocks with their tails fanned out in splendor, and rows of white chrysanthemums, Great Aunt Pei began to talk softly about her late husband. "Your Great Uncle Wu was not a warrior like other men, but he was still held in supreme respect because of his great learning. Learning that far surpassed the knowledge of books. Wu was

your father's tutor. I know it is hard to imagine the great General Tso as small boy." A smile broke the lines on her ancient face.

"One day Wu made Tso sit down and peel an onion. How he cried as he removed the outer layers. Wu took great delight in Tso's plight. He then grew serious as he spoke these words to your father: 'Remember what I tell you, there will be a time when your life will be surrounded by tears, but, as with the onion, the outer layers will peel away and you will discover the sweetness waiting for you.'"

Li was always enraptured by these stories and he took great pains to understand them. Great Aunt Pei continued, "I would say to Wu how proud I am to be the wife of the Court Scholar. He would only laugh and say, 'Do not praise my head, praise my feet. I am merely the most patient of men. While others get tired and walk away from knowledge, I remain standing.'"

"The oracle Yantz was my husband's best friend. Their friendship was so strong that when Wu died Yantz decided to give away his house and all of his possessions. He told me that only by living high in the mountains with his head in the clouds could he still feel close to his friend.

"These memories fill me with loss. Let us rest on a comfortable bench and observe silence." Observing silence was very important to her because, as she had said, "How else can you hear far away and long ago?"

Just then a messenger approached and made a ceremonial bow. "Greetings from the all powerful General Tso, Madam Pei. The general requests that you accompany his son to court. He will arrive at the head of his victorious army when the sun is about to disappear from the sky."

"Come Li, Char-in will be anxious to get you ready. You were worried he would miss your birthday," Great Aunt Pei said as she pinched his smiling cheeks.

Char-in was officially a slave but unofficially was a delightful big sister who took care of Li. He called her the "beauteous Char-in." She was skilled in the playing of the lute and in the singing of traditional songs. It was impossible to be bored in her company.

Char-in often played her music at the large open window in his bedroom. Li would hold his arm out very still, patiently waiting for a beautiful violet colored bird to perch.

They called the bird Great Uncle Wu and imagined that the magical oracle Yantz had gotten mad at Wu and changed him into a bird.

Li strained his neck outside the smaller north window, making it difficult for Char-in to get him dressed. "Please Li," she begged, "be obedient, you do not want to get me in trouble."

"I am sorry, Char-in, anticipation has made me impolite. Look, Char-in, here he comes! Isn't he glorious?"

It was a spectacle of which he never grew tired: His father at the head of row upon row of mounted soldiers, followed by a great number of archers and swordsmen. Each class of soldiers had his role to play in battle, his father often told him. The last rays of the afternoon sun reflected brilliantly off the General's armor. His father was truly born of the sun, Li thought. It was all too much for a seven year old to take in.

"I wonder what gifts I will receive this time?" said the high spirited Li. "Perhaps a new governess; that would be a nice change, what do you think?"

I think you love to tease this poor servant gir
answered Char-in. "Come you naught boy, v _
must go to court, where I will be forced to give
an unfavorable report to your father."

"Hey, who is the teaser now?" said a laughing Li.

The stone floor vibrated with the noisy clanging of armor. Li wondered how his father ever
surprised an enemy walking around like that.
Everyone sat down after the General reposed
in what had to be the biggest chair in the world.

Li knew the routine well. A procession of nervous elderly men would give reports to his father. Sometimes he would laugh or scowl, but
when he yelled it was like a huge rock hitting a
pool of water, scattering his advisors like bits
of driftwood onto the shore.

After Li made his required appearance at court,
Char-in led him by the hand back to the family
quarters. Char-in made supper for him and
Great Aunt Pei. Li picked at his food, clearly
too excited to eat.

Suddenly, the larger than life General Tso
burst into the room shouting, "My son, where
is my son?" Char-in backed out of the room

as quietly as a departing thought. A giant hand picked up Li and transported him into a fierce world. The General told Li of his great victories and how he had outwitted his enemies. He made it seem like the most fun anyone could possibly have. Then, the General realized he was not alone with his son. "My apologies, dear Aunt. I did not notice your presence." He gently kissed her hand. Aunt Pei had been sitting quietly in the far corner of the room enjoying the reunion.

"I did not wish to intrude. It is past an old woman's bedtime. I am truly happy to see you home safely, my nephew," she said as she walked out of the door.

The General and his son settled into a timeless evening with Li examining his gifts from far off lands. At last the General said, "I have such dreams for your, my son. Go to sleep, my precious Li. Tomorrow is a special day. For the first time you will see the world outside the castle grounds. When you are grown you will be the ruler of this land, and the people must get used to their future leader."

THE NEXT MORNING Li was outfitted to look like his father. "I feel like I am going to explode with pride on this day," he thought. Li's eyes were everywhere. He did not want to miss any new experience as he rode along next to his father at the head of a small detachment of soldiers.

They visited many villages and farms. The people always brought out food and water, showing the greatest respect. Li observed that they should dress better and eat more themselves, but who was he to tell people how to live?

The General was in an exalted mood as he contemplated the perfection of this day: a fine loyal army, a grateful citizenry, and a wonderful son. Surely all this was a divine reward for his exemplary life.

Without warning, a small thin girl stepped from behind a bush. So sudden was her appearance that it caused the General's horse to rear back on its hind legs. Fan-yar, the General's long time aide, leapt from his horse, sword in hand. Almost without thinking, Li quickly slid from his horse as well, and threw himself between the thin little girl and Fan-yar's angry sword. Fan-yar recoiled out of fear that he might hurt the son of his master.

The General roared, "You almost caused my horse to throw me!"

"I meant no harm," the little girl said in a strangely calm voice. "I was merely waiting to speak to you. You are the fierce General Tso of my dreams. I knew you were coming." The General was puzzled, but Li sensed danger and moved closer to the girl, feeling very protective.

Her eyes fixed solely on the General, she continued, "We are your people and we starve. I ask only that you feed us before it is too late."

She stood perfectly still, waiting for an answer. A slight breeze stirred the tattered remains of her clothes. Thin fabric clung to skeletal limbs. In the long, uncomfortable silence that followed, a new awareness slowly dawned in Li's tear-blurred eyes.

Fan-yar finally broke the spell with a derisive challenge. "From what spring bubbles such courage, beggar girl?"

"Courage? You speak of courage? This is a word used by those with possessions! I do not have anything! My wonderful father did not return from one of your victorious battles! My lovely mother died in the 'Year of the Great Sickness.' I am the last of my brothers and sisters. So what would you threaten to take from me, O Great General, that would fill me with fear? Do you covet this small bag of stones I keep close to my heart?" As she said this, she removed the little bag of stones and emptied them at the feet of General Tso's horse, one at a time, softly saying the name of each family member as they left her hand.

> Jian Wang
> Yun Ding
> Xiao Bao Wang
> Xiao Gao Wang
> Xiao Xiao Wang

"Now you have everything, even my memories." Her last words were spoken with such passion that she exhausted herself and began to cough uncontrollably.

Ignoring Fan-Yar's glare, Li took his lunch from his saddlebags and quickly led her to a small nearby hut. An old woman came out and Li gave her some coins that he had received as a birthday present. Then Li took hold of both of the little girl's hands and said, "I do not know how, but I swear by the Divine One who made us all that I will save you." He hurried back to rejoin his father before the General could send his soldiers after him.

The General was so shocked by his son's actions that for the first time in his adult life, he did not know what to do except return to the castle in stunned silence. Li's mind and heart were whirling with new images, experiences, and, for the first time in his young life, concerns.

That night, before bed, the only thing the General said was, "Perhaps I have neglected your training. I will assign Fan-yar to be your instructor. You will no longer be taught by your Aunt Pei." His father left abruptly. Li could tell he was still reeling from the day's events.

Char-in came in to tuck him in and hear him say his prayers. He told her of his extraordinary day. "You were very brave today. I have always loved you, but now I am also proud of you," she said.

In the middle of the night Li woke up, his face warm with tears. He walked over and sat in Great Aunt Pei's favorite chair by the fireplace. His promise to the little girl weighed heavily on his heart. He tried to calm himself, deriving some comfort from being in his aunt's chair.

He knelt in front of the north window. It was his habit in prayer to focus on one star. "I am only a seven-year-old boy. I wear what others tell me to wear and study what others tell me to study. O Divine One, because I have no power I must rely on you. Help me to fulfill the pledge I made today."

Suddenly his grief and frustration lifted, and Li felt light as a feather. He felt so much better that he had no trouble falling into a deep sleep.

The next morning Li awakened happy and joyous. Char-in who had been concerned about him was astonished at the change.

Clearly perplexed, she asked, "Have you kept your pledge? Do you know the answer about how to save the little girl and the people?"

"No, Char-in, I do not know the answer. I do know that last night I prayed for the first time."

"What is this, more teasing? We pray every night before going to bed," said Char-in.

"No, we say words every evening. Last night, I said a prayer, and I believe it was answered. In what manner I do not know. That is up to God."

Char-in stared in amazement. "I have never met your Great Uncle Wu, but from all the stories I have heard about him, I believe I have just heard his voice."

After that, Li's life changed. He saw less of Char-in and his Great Aunt Pei. Fan-yar filled his days with swords and strategies. At the end of the day he barely had enough energy to eat his supper and get undressed. His spirits remained high, which pleased his father, who attributed his son's mood to a love of soldiering.

Two weeks later, Char-in called on Madam Pei. "My lady, I am worried about Li," she confided. "He grows thinner each day. At first I thought it was because of his new training, but now I am convinced something is wrong. I know it sounds strange. He eats his meals but they do not nourish him."

"Have you told the General?" asked Aunt Pei.

"I am afraid the words would crumble in my throat," Char-in answered. "It has to be you."

THE NEXT MORNING, Madam Pei intruded on Li's training, much to Fan-yar's obvious disapproval. "I am taking my nephew for a walk in the garden," she told him.

"I must report this to the General," Fan-yar snapped.

"Do as you will," she answered.

As she and Li strolled, she said, "It has been too long since we breathed in the sweet mountain air together, my beloved nephew."

"The sweetness comes from you, not the garden, venerable aunt." Their hands clasped and Aunt Pei, feeling how thin Li's hand had become, knew that Char-in's fears were justified. A cold shiver shook her badly. They had a long talk with Li telling her everything about what was troubling him and how he had resolved it.

"I am ashamed to admit," she told him, "that what you say about the condition of the people is true. The people suffer. It has always been so, but that does not make it right. I could tell you that a woman's voice would not have been heard, but the truth is, I did not have the courage to speak. *Perhaps now I will,* she thought to herself, as she turned to return to the castle.

When they got back, General Tso was angrily pacing back and forth, waiting for them. With a slight bow to his aunt, he asked if he might see her in private. He told his son he would join him for supper. The General was clearly trying to contain himself as he explained to his revered aunt the importance of Li's training.

Aunt Pei finally spoke. "You see enemies hundreds of miles away, but you cannot see your son in the next room.

"What do you mean?"

"Li dies before your eyes while you vainly parade in your armor," she said bitingly. Tso's arms bulged in white hot anger, and he started to leave before he said or did something that would bring disgrace upon his family. In a softer voice, she called out to him, "Wait, let us calm ourselves. Our anger does not help Li."

She paused to let her inner fire die down. "His food is of no benefit to him. Each day he grows thinner. My anger at you for removing him from my care and instruction has blinded me from seeing Li's condition. Do not let your anger at me keep you from seeing the truth. Go to him, my nephew."

General Tso headed towards his son's room, unable to believe that anyone or anything would dare to threaten the life of his son. When he arrived, he quietly slipped into a dark corner to watch his beloved son. He observed as Li was barely able to lift his chest armor over his head. He was shocked at the thinness his arms and the clear definition of his tiny ribs which were barely covered by a thin layer of skin.

In a quivering whisper he said, "What kind of father am I that I had to be told that my son was in such a condition?" The General stood in the shadows, tears flowing down his cheeks. "All these years watching men die in battle, and I felt nothing. What kind of man am I?"

Char-in entered by the servant's door, but the only light came from the fireplace, so the General remained unnoticed in the shadows. "How tenderly she assists my son with his night

65

clothes, more like a mother than a servant. I have never appreciated this girl before," the General thought.

"Li, I too cannot stop thinking about the little girl. I believe with all my heart that you will save her. When you do would you please give her this small poem and tell her that she is my heroine forever." Char-in gently covered his frail form with blankets while she talked to him.

"Please read it to me," whispered a very weak Li. "I do not have the strength to hold up a single word."

Tell Me A Story

Tell me it's the warm touch of morning, not the cold grip of midnight.
Tell me there is not a cloud in the soundless sky when the rain is blinding and the thunder deafening.
Tell me I have a home in heaven with shimmering vases of love in every room.
Go ahead — tell me.

THE TRUST

"It is truly a beautiful poem, Char-in. Perhaps you can set it to a melody and sing it to her?"

"Yes, I would be honored," replied Char-in.

Char-in put Li's clothes away and set out what he would wear in the morning. She turned around to say good night, but Li was already asleep. She went to the window where Li liked to say his prayers and raised her hands to the stars. She kissed her fingers and touched the starlight. "O divine One, I love you, but I confess that I love Li more. He is my child. He is my brother. He is my friend. Do not take him from me."

General Tso waited until Char-in had returned to her room to step out of the shadows.

He put some more wood on the fire and then, sitting on the chair beside Li's bed, he gently took his son's hand in his own. He was confused and terrified as never before.

Just then, Li began to toss and turn. Beads of sweat appeared on his brow, and his hands gripped his father's with a strange power.

Li began to mumble, "But I have not broken my pledge. You must hold out a little while longer. Please do not give up, you will be saved...." The grip of Li's hand actually began to hurt his father's hand.

"What magic is this?" whispered the dumb-founded General to himself. Finally Li slipped into a deep, exhausted sleep and General Tso was able to move his hand.

The next day, the General decided not to change the boy's routine, but to summon the court doctors for their opinion. Maybe they would find a cure and he would not have to alarm the child.

Different remedies were added to Li's food and Char-in was instructed to see that he ate everything on his plate. Char-in confided to Aunt Pei. "I don't know how much longer I can continue. The pain in my heart is so intense. What I do not understand is that Li is at peace and grows happier by the moment. It's almost as if he knows something that is beyond us."

The most respected healer was chosen by the rest of the doctors to give a report to the General. "Great General Tso, the boy's sickness is not of this world. He eats his food, but it is as if he is consuming air."

The doctors stood in silent fear of their lives.

"I believe in what you say," said Madam Pei, who had just entered. She quickly approached the General. "Come at once. Li has collapsed."

As they entered Li's bedroom, Fan-yar was lifting him into bed and taking off his uniform. Char-in was crying and could hardly look at the boy. "Father, I think I need to rest today," Li said, "but I will resume my training tomorrow."

"Yes, yes, my son. Just try to rest. I will stay by your side."

Everyone left the two alone.

The General thought to himself, "If all I can do is stay close to him then that's what I will do."

MEANWHILE, Aunt Pei had her own idea. She left the castle at great speed in her carriage, accompanied by her personal guard. Outside the city they took the mountain road that seemed to go straight up into the clouds. When they could go no higher and the horses were begging for a rest, they came to a small stone house.

The soldiers steadied Madam Pei on each arm as she made her way through the swirling mountain winds. Her eyes shifted for a moment to take in the astonishing view, but she had not come to revel in nature.

Feeling her new found bravery coursing through her arteries, she shouted, "Oracle Yantz! Rise! Do not sleep away your few remaining days."

Yantz appeared at the doorway of his hut. He was unusually small and also obviously blind.

"Those must be the dulcet tones of my best friend's wife. Come in Madam Pei, the winds are too strong for me to venture out today," Yantz said in a cheerful voice.

"I am sorry old friend. I did not know you had lost your eyesight," she said in a shy voice.

"Merely a trade I have made. I will make many more as my time grows nearer," Yantz joked wisely.

Madam Pei smiled. His words reminded her of Wu. Beneath the humor always lurked great wisdom.

"This is not the most convenient place for those who wish to consult you," Madam Pei said, her eyes avoiding his stare.

"Your long absence from my door has more to do with climbing the mountain in your own heart rather that this puny hill we stand on. It is the memory of Wu that I awaken within you," he said.

The honesty brought tears to her eyes, and they hugged. "Your tears are contagious, sweet sister."

"Help me to save my nephew Li. We don't have much time," she said in a raspy voice.

"Of all the people in this world I would want to help, he is the most important to me, for he possesses the qualities of our Wu. I have been expecting you," Yantz said warmly.

"So you know, Yantz?"

"Not all. Enough to know Li's prayer is being answered. I suspect the soil of his soul is being tilled for a great harvest in the future. I hear the words Li hears and the power they contain forces me to my knees:

"'Tell the rich of the midnight sighing of the poor, lest heedlessness lead them into the path of destruction, and deprive them of the Tree of Wealth....The poor in your midst are my trust, guard ye my trust and be not intent only on your own ease.'"*

"In my mind I see two little hands strongly entwined. This bond is unbreakable. They cannot be separated. You see the evident meaning, Madam Pei?"

"Yes, I do! You have proved invaluable. I must hurry back to the castle," she cried.

*Bahá'u'lláh, The Hidden Words, Persian #49 and #54

UPON HER RETURN from the mountain, Madam Pei strode across the great hall with a new purpose and power animating her.

She saw her nephew Tso, and for some reason she recalled to herself the story of the onion... and she understood.

In a whisper, General Tso said, "Revered Aunt, I cannot save him. My strong arms cannot save him, my armies cannot save him. Show me an enemy I can see and touch. I vow to defeat such an enemy even at the cost of my own life. But this," his voice rose on a wave of tears. After a long pause he said, "I did not know such pain existed," he concluded.

"If you are willing to die for your son then you should also be willing to live for him," she said, her hands gently encouraging him to follow her. When they reached Li's bedroom, Char-in was playing a wonderful melody on her lute and a smile was on Li's lips.

Still holding Tso's hand, she gently laid her other hand on Li's arm and drew them together. "You are the people in this world I love the most," she said solemnly. "You must listen and understand."

"First, dear nephew," she said to the general, "hand me your sword." Amazingly, he complied at once. She then threw it out the north window, right into the moat. "There is no enemy attacking your son! If you spend your life looking for enemies you will never find the friend! What has happened here is as natural as rainfall and sunshine. A child's prayer has been answered. In his heart, Li has continued to hold the hand of the starving little girl who approached you weeks ago. Through her he holds the hands of all the people of our kingdom."

She paused and looked into her nephew's eyes.

"Tso, do you really want to save the life of your son?"

"Yes, with all my heart!" was the father's reply.

Madam Pei took a deep breath and said, "Then you must save the lives of all your people. If you do not want to see your son starve to death, then do not let your people starve. Li's fate is now joined to theirs and there is no power on earth that can separate him from them."

Her words struck the general with the force of authority and the power of truth. Through his mind flashed the memories of a hundred scenes of battle and a thousand scenes of poverty, and on each face in every scene he saw the tender smile of his beloved son. Overwhelmed, he fell to his knees at Li's side and gently took a frail hand in his. "Of all the battles I have ever fought," he said, "this one will be the most difficult. But I pledge to you by my very soul that I will do my best."

Then, like the great commander that he was, he stood, wiped the tears from his eyes, and strode quickly from the room, bellowing orders to his advisors. "Get me the figures on our grain reserves.... We will need wagons...."

TIME PASSED and General Tso became a true leader and a compasionate father – interested in the well-being of all his people. The goodness of General Tso became legend and his kingdom became the envy of all peoples.

Li grew up and married the little girl. You see, he never did let go of her hand! She grew up to become the most famous woman of her time – a fame that spread beyond vast deserts, over the highest mountains, and through the thickest of walled cities. The mother of the nameless ones is what she was called by the poorest and richest alike.

Even now, if you should be able to visit the great statue of her likeness, you will see little children leaving small stones at her feet.

THE TRUST

Here is a translation of one of her most loved poems:

The Nameless Ones

They are falling from the heavens
They are falling in the darkest hours
    before the dawn
Bits of coral
Drops of pearls
Jagged diamonds
And smooth pieces of ebony
Catch them!
Catch all you can!
Dry their mother's red tears
And hold them until the sun comes up.

The End